Ingredients for a Healthy Life

GREAT GRAIN Recipes

Gareth Stevens
PUBLISHING

By Kristen Rajczak

Please visit our website, www.garethstevens.com. For a free color catalog of all our high-quality books, call toll free 1-800-542-2595 or fax 1-877-542-2596.

Library of Congress Cataloging-in-Publication Data

Rajczak, Kristen.
Great grain recipes / by Kristen Rajczak.
  p. cm. — (Ingredients for a healthy life)
Includes index.
ISBN 978-1-4824-0570-5 (pbk.)
ISBN 978-1-4824-3327-2 (6-pack)
ISBN 978-1-4824-0569-9 (library binding)
1. Cereals as food — History — Juvenile literature. 2. Cooking (Cereals) — Juvenile literature. 3. Grain – Juvenile literature. I. Rajczak, Kristen. II. Title.
TX393.R35 2014
641.3—dc23

First Edition

Published in 2015 by
Gareth Stevens Publishing
111 East 14th Street, Suite 349
New York, NY 10003

Copyright © 2015 Gareth Stevens Publishing

Designer: Andrea Davison-Bartolotta
Editor: Kristen Rajczak

Photo credits: Cover, back cover, pp. 1, 3, 9, 13, 15, 17, 21–24 (bread background) Kheng Guan Toh/Shutterstock.com; cover, p. 1 (bread) Tim UR/Shutterstock.com; cover, p. 1 (cookies) Anna Hoychuk/Shutterstock.com; cover, p. 1 (salad) Sofy/Shutterstock.com; p. 4 mexrix/Shutterstock.com; p. 5 (main) wavebreakmedia/Shutterstock.com; p. 5 (inset) Igor Strukov/Shutterstock.com; p. 6 Dorling Kindersley/Getty Images; p. 7 (main) Egyptian/The Bridgeman Art Library/Getty Images; p. 7 (inset) DEA/G. Dagli Orti/Getty Images; p. 8 oksix/Shutterstock.com; p. 9 Anna Sedneva/Shutterstock.com; p. 10 TatjanaRittner/Shutterstock.com; p. 11 Elena Schweitzer/Shutterstock.com; p. 13 (sesame seeds) Pinkcandy/Shutterstock.com; p. 13 (puffed rice) Swapan Photography/Shutterstock.com; p. 13 (almonds) Louella938/Shutterstock.com; p. 13 (pumpkin seeds) Nagel Oleg/Shutterstock.com; p. 14 M. Unal Ozmen/Shutterstock.com; p. 15 Marie C Fields/Shutterstock.com; p. 16 Imageman/Shutterstock.com; p. 17 zoryanchik/Shutterstock.com; pp. 18, 21 (girl, arrows) iStockphoto/Thinkstock; p. 19 (main) Ingram Publishing/Thinkstock; p. 19 (inset) Lena Gabrilovich/Shutterstock.com; p. 20 ChameleonsEye/Shutterstock.com.

Printed in the United States of America

CPSIA compliance information: Batch #CS15GS: For further information contact Gareth Stevens, New York, New York at 1-800-542-2595.

Contents

! Recipes in this book may use knives, mixers, and hot stove tops. Ask for an adult's help when using these tools.

Words in the glossary appear in **bold** type the first time they are used in the text.

Start Your Day with Grains

Imagine you could eat anything you wanted for breakfast. What would you choose? You could have a muffin, pancakes, or a big bowl of oatmeal. Or would you rather just have your usual bowl of cornflakes? Whatever you'd pick, all these breakfast foods have something in common—they contain grains!

Grains are a big group of plants grown for food that are called cereal crops. Wheat, oats, and corn are just a few cereal crops. They're a common part of a healthy, tasty **diet**!

Do You Have Allergies?

The **recipes** in this book may use **ingredients** that contain or have come into contact with nuts, gluten, dairy products, and other common causes of **allergies**. If you have any food allergies, please ask a parent or teacher for help when cooking and tasting!

The word "cereal" comes from the Roman goddess of grains and farming, Ceres. That's why grains are called cereal crops.

wheat field

5

Long Ago

Cereal crops belong to the grass family. The grains people eat are the seeds of these crops.

People have been growing and eating grains for thousands of years. Barley may be the grain that's been grown the longest, with a history of **cultivation** going back as many as 10,000 years! It's likely that both wheat and barley were first grown in the Fertile Crescent. This is the name for an area in the Middle East that includes the Nile, the Tigris, and the Euphrates Rivers.

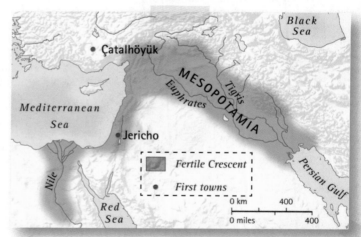

CHEW ON THIS!

Flour is one of the most common ways people eat grains. Flour is most often made of the seeds of cereal crops ground into a fine powder.

The ancient Egyptians grew wheat for dozens of different types of bread.

ancient bread makers

Keeping It Together

Grain seeds, or kernels, are most commonly eaten after they've been **processed**. This includes the removal of the outer part of the seed that can't be eaten. The kernels may then be cracked or broken into smaller pieces or pressed flat in giant rollers so they cook faster.

Whole grains are those that still contain the three main parts of the kernel: the bran, the germ, and the endosperm. Even though they've been pressed flat, oats are a good example of a whole grain.

CHEW ON THIS!

White flour, white bread, and most crackers are made with refined grains. That means the grain has been processed so much that it's lost many of its **nutrients**. Eating whole grains whenever you can is the best choice for your diet.

Sweet Oat Quick Bread

makes one loaf, about 10 servings

Ingredients:

1 cup old-fashioned rolled oats or quick-cooking oats, plus 2 tablespoons

1 1/3 cups whole-wheat flour or white whole-wheat flour

1 cup all-purpose flour

2 1/4 teaspoons baking powder

1/4 teaspoon baking soda

1 1/4 teaspoons salt

8 ounces low-fat plain yogurt

1 egg

1/4 cup canola oil

1/4 cup clover honey or other mild honey

3/4 cup skim milk

Directions:

1. Preheat oven to 375 degrees.
2. Spray a bread loaf pan with cooking spray. Sprinkle 1 tablespoon of oats in the bottom of the pan. Shake the pan slowly from side to side to coat the sides and bottom of the pan with the oats. Set aside another tablespoon to top the loaf with.
3. Stir the whole-wheat and all-purpose flours together with the baking powder, baking soda, and salt.
4. In another bowl, use a fork to combine the remaining 1 cup of oats, yogurt, egg, oil, and honey. Blend in the milk.
5. Add the wet oat mixture to the flours until just mixed.
6. Pour the batter into the loaf pan. Sprinkle the last tablespoon of oats on the top.
7. Bake for about 40 to 50 minutes, or until a toothpick inserted into the middle comes out clean and the top is golden brown.
8. Let cool for about 15 minutes. Run a knife around the edges of the pan to loosen the bread and turn it out to cool completely.

Have you ever made your own bread? Some breads use **yeast**, which can be time-consuming and hard to work with. This bread is a bit easier, and it gives you a dose of whole grains with whole-wheat flour and oats.

Why Whole Grains?

All grains deliver carbohydrates, which the body uses for energy. But when eaten "whole," grains can give you so much more!

The biggest part of the kernel is the endosperm. It's full of carbohydrates, **protein**, and some vitamins and minerals. The germ also contains protein, vitamins, and minerals, as well as healthy **fats**. Whole grains provide fiber, which is plant matter the body can't break down and uses to move food and waste through the body. Much of that is found in the bran.

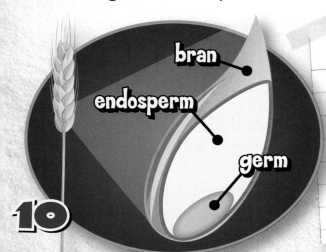

bran

endosperm

germ

CHEW ON THIS!

Vitamins and minerals are nutrients the body needs to work well. While companies that make products with refined grains add some into their food, whole grains are a better source and have more protein and fiber.

When grains are refined, they commonly lose their bran and germ. So, about 25 percent of the kernel's protein is lost, too.

Switch It Up!

You can easily replace refined grains with whole grains in your diet! Here are some simple swaps that will help you gain the health benefits of whole grains:

- Eat a bran muffin instead of a pastry.

- Make whole-wheat toast instead of a plain bagel.

- Cook brown rice instead of white rice.

- Use oatmeal or crushed bran cereal instead of bread crumbs.

- Choose whole-wheat pasta instead of regular.

If you're unsure about a grain product, check the ingredient list. The first ingredient should be whole-wheat or whole-grain flour.

CHEW ON THIS!

Grain products, such as cereals, pastas, and breads, often have many ingredients. In addition to looking for those made with whole-wheat or whole-grain flour, choose grain products with a short ingredient list of things you recognize, like yeast, water, and milk.

Super Grain Party Mix

makes 8 cups

Ingredients:

4 cups whole-grain cereal (not flakes)
2 cups puffed brown rice cereal
1 cup sliced almonds
1/4 cup raw sesame seeds
1 cup raw pumpkin seeds
1 tablespoon sesame oil
1/4 cup soy sauce
1 tablespoon Worcestershire sauce
1/2 cup canola oil
1/2 teaspoon chili powder
1/4 teaspoon salt

Instead of chips and dip, serve this homemade, whole-grain party treat. Your friends will love trying something new you've made!

Directions:

1. Preheat oven to 300 degrees.
2. Mix the whole-grain cereal, puffed rice cereal, almonds, sesame seeds, and pumpkin seeds together.
3. In a separate bowl, use a whisk or fork to blend the sesame oil, soy sauce, Worcestershire sauce, canola oil, chili powder, and salt.
4. Pour the liquid and spice mix over the cereal, almonds, and seeds. Toss to coat.
5. Spread the mixture onto a cookie sheet and bake for 30 minutes, stirring about every 10 minutes.
6. Remove from the oven and allow to cool and set before eating.

sesame seeds

puffed rice cereal

pumpkin seeds

almonds

Get Baking

When baking, it's a good idea to start using whole-wheat flour instead of white flour. It can give a yummy nutty flavor to pancakes, breads, and homemade crackers. Whole-wheat flour can make baked goods too thick or heavy, though. One way to fix this is to use half whole-wheat and half white flour in a recipe.

There's another great choice: white whole-wheat flour. White wheat has the same nutritional benefits as the more common "red" wheat, but gives baked goods a lighter flavor and **texture**.

whole-wheat flour

CHEW ON THIS!

Some recipes call for flour made from almonds, coconuts, or beans!

Buttery Sugar Cookies

makes about 2 dozen cookies, depending on size of cookie cutters

Ingredients:

1 cup white whole-wheat flour
1/2 cup all-purpose flour
1 teaspoon baking powder
1/4 teaspoon salt
3 tablespoons butter
1 tablespoon canola oil
1 egg
1/2 cup light brown sugar
1/2 teaspoon vanilla extract

Baking is one of the most fun ways to use grains! This recipe for sugar cookies has mostly whole-wheat flour so you can have a treat that tastes good and is better for you.

Directions:

1. Use a fork to mix together the flours, baking powder, and salt.
2. Melt the butter in a small pan on the stove. Heat until it's lightly browned and smells very buttery, about 1 minute, stirring it a few times so that it doesn't burn. Remove from heat and let the butter cool slightly.
3. Mix together the browned butter, oil, egg, brown sugar, and vanilla.
4. Add the flour mixture to the wet ingredients a little at a time until well mixed.
5. Spread out a big sheet of plastic wrap. Make the dough into a ball and place it on the plastic wrap, and then wrap it up. Place the dough in the refrigerator for at least an hour.
6. Preheat the oven to 350 degrees. Line two cookie sheets with parchment paper or grease them with cooking spray.
7. Sprinkle flour on the counter. Unwrap the dough and turn it out onto the flour.
8. Use a rolling pin to roll out the dough to about 1/8 inch thick. Cut out cookies with cookie cutters or an upside-down glass and place them on the cookie sheets.
9. Bake for 6 to 8 minutes, or until the edges look slightly brown.
10. Let the cookies cool for a few minutes before removing them from the sheets.

Barley Boost

Many whole grains can be eaten in ways similar to rice or pasta. But make sure you've got a quick-cooking kind or you have the time to prepare them. Depending on which grain you've chosen, whole grains can take 30 minutes to an hour to cook.

Barley is one of these slow-cooking grains—and it's worth it! Alone, barley is chewy and nutty. You can eat it with vegetables or mix it with yogurt and fruit in place of oatmeal.

barley

CHEW ON THIS!

Barley is sold as flour, flakes, and, perhaps most commonly, in kernels. It's a good source of protein and fiber as well as two of the B vitamins.

Fresh and Tasty Barley Salad

makes about 8 servings

Ingredients:

Salad:

3 cups vegetable stock

1 cup barley

1/2 cup onion, sliced thin

1 bunch radishes, sliced

1 cucumber, peeled, seeded, and diced

1 red bell pepper, seeded and sliced

1 large carrot, chopped small or grated

1/2 cup chopped fresh mint (or 1/4 cup dried mint)

1/2 cup chopped fresh parsley

Dressing:

3 tablespoons extra-virgin olive oil

3 tablespoons fresh lemon juice

3–4 cloves garlic, mashed

pinch of salt

Directions:

1. Bring the vegetable stock to a boil in a pan on the stove. Add the barley and cover. Lower the heat and allow the barley to simmer for about 45 minutes, or until the stock has been mostly **absorbed**.
2. Drain the barley well. Place it in a bowl.
3. In another bowl, combine the extra-virgin olive oil, lemon juice, salt, and mashed garlic, and mix well.
4. Pour the dressing over the barley and stir to coat.
5. Allow the barley to cool. Then, add the onions, radishes, cucumber, red pepper, carrot, parsley, and mint. Stir together and chill in the refrigerator before serving.

This barley salad can easily be made with other hearty whole grains, such as wheat berries. The veggies in this recipe make it perfect for a dinner side dish or summer picnic salad.

Ancient Grains

Are you tired of oatmeal and rice? There are so many more kinds of grains out there to try! Some, such as spelt and farro, are called "ancient grains" because they've been cultivated for so long.

Another group to try is known as "pseudograins." These grains aren't in the same plant family as cereal grains, but are similar nutritionally and can be cooked in many of the same ways. Amaranth is one popular pseudograin, as are quinoa (KEEN-wah) and buckwheat.

farro

CHEW ON THIS!

Corn is a grain, too! That means when you enjoy a bowl of popcorn while watching a movie, you're eating a serving of whole grains.

Corn isn't just yellow. Throughout history, people have grown red, blue, pink, and even black corn!

Are You Gluten Free?

People with celiac disease can't eat wheat, barley, and rye products. Their body reacts badly to gluten, a protein found in these grains.

While there's no cure for celiac disease, doctors have found that a gluten-free diet helps to manage the **digestive** problems the illness causes. What grains can those with celiac disease eat? They can chow down on rice, corn, millet, and buckwheat, among others—as long as they know it hasn't come into contact with grains containing gluten.

CHEW ON THIS!

In a person with celiac disease, the small intestine is harmed by the body's reaction to gluten and can't properly absorb nutrients.

GLUTEN FREE

Healthy Reasons to Eat Grains

Vitamins and minerals in grains provide the body with what it needs to grow and stay healthy!

Whole grains are good sources of protein, which helps build muscle.

Whole grains are full of fiber! That keeps your digestive system working well.

The carbohydrates in grains give the body energy.

Glossary

absorb: to take in

allergy: a body's sensitivity to usually harmless things in the surroundings, such as dust, pollen, or mold

cultivation: having to do with raising crops by caring for the land and plants as they grow

diet: the food one usually eats

digestive: having to do with the breaking down of food inside the body so it can be used

fat: one of the basic nutrients that supplies energy to the body

ingredient: a food that is mixed with other foods

nutrient: something a living thing needs to grow and stay alive

processed: changed from its original state

protein: a nutrient in many types of food that the body uses to grow, repair tissues, and stay healthy

recipe: an explanation of how to make food

texture: the structure, feel, and appearance of something

yeast: a product made of tiny fungi that help raise bread dough

For More Information

BOOKS

Price, Pam. *Cool Quick Breads: Easy Recipes for Kids to Bake.* Edina, MN: ABDO Publishing Company, 2010.

Reinke, Beth Bence. *The Grains Group.* Mankato, MN: Child's World, 2013.

WEBSITES

How It's Made: Bread
science.howstuffworks.com/innovation/5125-how-its-made-bread-video.htm
Watch a video about how bread is made in a factory, from flour to loaf.

Kids Kitchen: Whole Grains
pubs.ext.vt.edu/348/348-837/348-837_pdf.pdf
Use this helpful document to choose the healthiest grains for your diet.

Index